George
CLASS CLOWN
How Do You Pee in Space?

For Ian and Mandy: Never stop reaching for the stars!—NK

For Faith—out of this world super agent!—AB

GROSSET & DUNLAP
Published by the Penguin Group
Penguin Group (USA) LLC, 375 Hudson Street, New York, New York 10014, USA

USA | Canada | UK | Ireland | Australia | New Zealand | India | South Africa | China

penguin.com
A Penguin Random House Company

Text copyright © 2014 by Nancy Krulik. Illustrations copyright © 2014 by Aaron Blecha. All rights reserved. Published by Grosset & Dunlap, a division of Penguin Young Readers Group, 345 Hudson Street, New York, New York 10014. GROSSET & DUNLAP is a trademark of Penguin Group (USA) LLC. Printed in the USA.

Library of Congress Cataloging-in-Publication Data is available.

ISBN 978-0-448-46113-7   10 9 8 7 6 5 4 3 2

George Brown, CLASS CLOWN

How Do You Pee in Space?

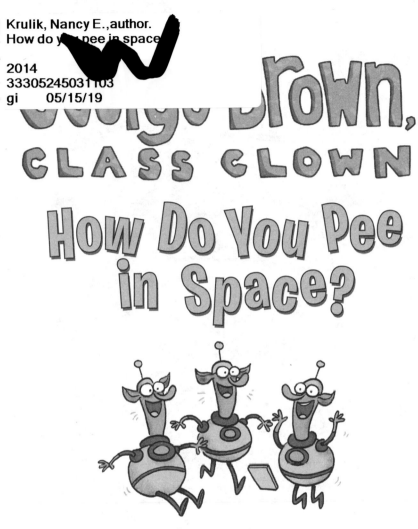

by Nancy Krulik

illustrated by Aaron Blecha

Grosset & Dunlap
An Imprint of Penguin Group (USA) LLC

Chapter 1

"Remember, class, we're not the only school visiting the planetarium today, so I expect you to be on your best **field-trip** behavior," Mrs. Kelly said as she led the Edith B. Sugarman fourth-graders into the Beaver Brook Planetarium. "Your *very* best field-trip behavior," she added, looking straight at George Brown.

George frowned. Teachers always looked at him when they said **stuff** like that. He sat down at the end of the row and stared up at the round ceiling. Mrs. Kelly had nothing to worry about with him. He wasn't going to cause any trouble during the field trip.

At least he was going to *try* not to cause any trouble.

Just then, the lights went down. Bright stars **twinkled** overhead. A recording of a man's deep, booming voice came over a loudspeaker.

"The stars in our night sky have been burning for centuries," he said. "The same stars we see now were viewed by the pharaohs of **ancient** Egypt and the philosophers of ancient Greece and Rome. Those people long ago noticed that the stars were grouped together in shapes, which we call **constellations**."

George frowned and squirmed around in his seat. *Bo-ring.*

"These stars form the Big Dipper," the voice continued, as lines connecting some stars appeared on the ceiling of the planetarium. "And these form the Little Dipper."

George wiggled around in his seat some more. Was this ever going to get more interesting?

"And these stars . . ."

The man on the loudspeaker was saying something else, but George wasn't paying attention. **He couldn't.** Not while there was something much more exciting going on—right inside his belly.

Bing-bong. Ping-pong.

There were **bubbles** in there! Not just your usual, run-of-the-mill kind of bubbles. Strong, powerful bubbles. Bubbles that slam-danced against George's spleen and kickboxed with his kidneys. Bubbles that hip-hopped on his heart and leaped to his larynx. Bubbles that could **burst** out of him and . . .

BUUURP!

Just then, George let out a powerful burp. A super burp. A burp so loud, and so strong, it could knock **the Big Dipper** right out of the sky.

Alex looked over at George. "Dude, no!" he shouted.

Dude, yes! The magical super burp had escaped. And now, whatever **the burp** wanted to do, George had to do.

"This constellation is Draco," the

recorded voice said. "The dragon."

"ROAR!" Suddenly the burp made George roar like a **fire-breathing** dragon. "ROAR!"

A few of the kids in the planetarium laughed. None of the teachers did.

"And this is Lepus, the hare," the recorded voice continued.

That was all the burp had to hear. The next thing George knew, he had leaped out of his seat and was **hippity-hoppitying** around the planetarium.

"George, sit down!" Mrs. Kelly scolded.

George *wanted* to sit down. But George wasn't in charge now. The burp was.

"And this is Pisces, the fish," the recorded voice continued.

Uh-oh! Suddenly the magical super burp made George's whole body start

flipping and flopping, like a fish out of water. George sucked in his cheeks and made a fish face. Then he leaped over the seats and planted **a big, wet fish kiss** right on Louie's cheek!

"Yuck!" Louie shouted. He wiped George's **spit** from his face. "Get off of me!"

Yuck was right. The last thing George ever wanted to do was kiss Louie Farley. Stupid super burp. It was going crazy. **George was helpless** to stop it.

The kids from the other schools laughed hard. Their teachers tried to shush them.

The kids from George's school were laughing, too. But Mrs. Kelly wasn't trying to quiet them. She was too busy trying to stop George.

A teacher was **no match for the burp**. So George kept hippity-hoppitying and flipping and flopping, and . . .

Pop! George felt something burst in the bottom of his belly. All the air rushed out of him. It was like someone had popped a balloon inside him. The super burp was gone. But George was still in the planetarium. And he was in **trouble**.

"Young man!"

George turned around to see a man in a blue uniform coming up behind him. He was wearing a little badge that read SECURITY.

"You'll have to come with me," the security guard said. "You can wait for your class at the security desk."

Make that *big* trouble.

As he left the planetarium, George looked up at the ceiling one more time. Stupid stars. **They weren't lucky** for George at all. In fact, it was a star that had caused him all the trouble in the first place.

It started when George and his family first arrived in Beaver Brook. George's dad was in the army, so the family moved around a lot. By now, George understood that first days at school could be pretty rotten. But *this* first day was **the absolute rottenest**.

In his old school, George had been the class clown. He was always pulling pranks and making jokes. But George had promised himself that things were going to be different at Edith B. Sugarman Elementary School. He was turning over a new leaf. **No more pranks.** No more whoopee cushions or spitballs shot through straws. No more bunny ears behind people's heads. No more goofing on teachers when their backs were turned.

But being the well-behaved new kid didn't earn George any friends. None of the kids even seemed to know he was there. It was like he was the invisible George Brown.

That night, George's parents took him out to Ernie's Ice Cream Emporium. While they were sitting outside and George was finishing his root beer float, a **shooting star** flashed across the sky. So

George made a wish.

I want to make kids laugh—but not get into trouble.

Unfortunately, the star was gone before George could finish the wish. So only half came true—the first half.

A minute later, George had **a funny feeling in his belly**. It was like there were hundreds of tiny bubbles bouncing around in there. The bubbles hopped up and down and all around. They ping-ponged their way into his chest, and bing-bonged their way up into his throat.

And then . . .

George let out a big burp. A *huge* burp. A SUPER burp!

The super burp was loud, and it was *magic*.

Suddenly George lost control of his arms and legs. It was like they had minds of their own. His hands grabbed straws and **stuck them up his nose** like a walrus. His feet jumped up on the table and started dancing the hokey pokey. Everyone at Ernie's started laughing—except George's parents, who were **covered in the ice cream** he'd kicked over while he was dancing.

The magical super burp came back lots of times after that, and every time it did, bubble, bubble, George was in trouble. Like the time the burp burst out in the middle of Mr. Stubbs's barbershop and made George spray mountains of **sticky shaving cream** all over the place.

Or the time it made him paint a mural on the wall of the auditorium during the school art show. The burp hadn't used paint; it used **jelly-doughnut jelly**. But it was George who had to clean it up—while everyone else went out for ice cream.

None of the trouble had been George's fault. The burp was to blame. But George didn't tell anyone that. Who would believe him?

The only other person in Beaver Brook who knew about the super burp was Alex. George hadn't told him about it—Alex was just **so smart** that he figured it out himself. Luckily for George, Alex wasn't just smart. He was a good friend, too. He'd promised not to tell anyone about it. And he hadn't.

Better yet, Alex had promised to help George find a cure to get rid of the burps once and for all. So far the boys had tried a lot of things—everything from minty candy canes to **onion-flavored milk shakes**—but nothing had worked. The burp had beaten them all.

As he sat down next to the security desk to wait for his class, George stared down at the floor. A **huge cockroach** was crawling along it.

George yawned. Watching the cockroach *outside* the planetarium was even more boring than watching the star show *inside* the planetarium.

Still, it was probably a lot safer for him to be out here than around all those stars. After all, cockroaches might be **creepy-crawly**, but they didn't cause a guy any trouble. How could they? Who would ever make a wish on a crawling cockroach?

Chapter 2

Blah blah blah blah blah.

That wasn't what Mrs. Kelly was saying, but it was pretty much what George was hearing. It was Tuesday morning, the day after the field trip, and Mrs. Kelly was assigning the vocabulary words for the week. Constellation. **Meteor.** Nebula. *Blah blah blah.* George wasn't the only one who was having a **tough time** listening. He could tell when he looked around at the other kids.

Sage was busy chewing on a strand of her hair.

Julianna was staring out the window.

Louie was pushing the button on the top of his pen up and down.

Mike had his head on his desk. George was pretty sure **he was snoring**.

The only person in the room who actually seemed interested in what Mrs. Kelly was saying was Alex. He loved science.

But to George it still sounded like *blah blah blah blah.*

That is, until Mrs. Kelly said, "Who would like to meet **an astronaut**?"

Wow! Now *that* sounded cool. George's hand shot up without him even thinking about it—and without the help of a magical super burp. Everyone else raised their hands, too.

"I knew you would be excited," Mrs.

Kelly said. "That's why I'm thrilled to tell you that Major Chet Minor, a real astronaut, is coming to our fourth-grade assembly Thursday. He's going to tell us what it's like to **travel in space**."

Whoa! George thought. *A real astronaut!* This was definitely not *blah blah blah.*

"And to make it even more **special**, one fourth-grader is going to interview Major Minor on our school's TV station during morning announcements," Mrs. Kelly said.

"I'll do it," Louie volunteered. "I'd be a great interviewer."

"What makes you a great interviewer?" George asked him.

"I have a new suit," Louie said. **"Interviewers wear suits."**

George rolled his eyes. *Oh brother.*

"Actually, we're holding a contest to choose the interviewer," Mrs. Kelly told the class. "To enter, you have to submit three questions you would like to ask Major Minor. You should also try to do really well in tomorrow's Statewide Physical-Fitness Challenge. Half of your score will be based on **how strong** your questions are, and the other half will be based on how well you do on the challenge."

George was confused. "What does the

physical-fitness challenge have to do with anything?" he asked Mrs. Kelly. "You don't have to be fit to do an interview."

"No, you don't," Mrs. Kelly agreed. "But you do have to be fit to go to the **Space Adventurers Program**. Major Minor is giving the winner a free scholarship for a week there."

"He's taking one of us up into *space*?" Mike asked.

"No," Alex said. "The Space Adventurers Program is like a camp. The kids who go there get to do astronaut training **just like the real astronauts do**. They have flight simulators, and a multi-axis trainer and . . ."

George grinned at his best buddy as he spoke. Alex sure made the Space Adventurers Program sound exciting. It would be really cool to spend a week there. It would also be pretty cool to get to interview a real-life astronaut. In fact, winning this contest would be **totally out of this world**!

"I sure hope I win," Alex said as he, Chris, and George took their trays over to the lunch table and sat down with the other fourth-graders. "I've been begging my parents to send me to the Space Adventurers Program, but they say it's too expensive."

Louie laughed. "Space Adventurers Program," he said. "Well, at least they named it right. S-A-P. **That place is for saps**."

"Don't you want to learn what it's like to be in space?" Alex asked Louie.

"Sure," Louie replied. "But I'm going to learn about space by *being* in space."

"You can't do that," George argued.

"Only astronauts can go up in space."

"Shows what you know," Louie told him. "You can do **anything you want** if you have enough money. There's a company that's building real space launchers and selling tickets on them to people like me."

"People like *you*?" Julianna wondered. "What's that supposed to mean?"

"Rich people," Louie replied. "I'm going to ask my dad to buy me a ticket on one of those launchers."

George looked at Alex. "Is there really a company selling tickets on a launcher?"

Alex nodded. "And it will **cost a lot more** than a week at the Space Adventurers Program. But I'd be happy just going to the camp."

"And talking face-to-face with a real-life astronaut," George added. "Don't forget that part."

"Major Chet Minor is **really famous**," Alex said. "I read about him in a science magazine. He spent time at the International Space Station. He's even walked around in space."

"I wonder if he's ever met any space aliens," George said.

Louie laughed so hard that he snorted and **milk came out of his nose**.

"What's so funny?" George asked him.

"You are," Louie answered. **"There's no such thing as aliens."**

"How do you know?" George asked.

"Because I've never met an alien," Louie said. "Neither has my brother, Sam."

"What does that prove?" George asked him.

"Think about it," Louie said. "Sam's the most **popular** kid in Beaver Brook Middle School. And I'm the most popular kid here. Everyone wants to be friends with a Farley. So if aliens had landed on Earth, they would have made it their business to meet one of us."

George didn't know how to answer that. There were so many **ridiculous** things about what Louie had just said he didn't know where to start.

"I'm going to start getting ready for the physical-fitness challenge right after school," George said, changing the subject. "That means sit-ups, push-ups, climbing—"

"The rope-climbing part of the Statewide Physical-Fitness Challenge is really hard," Alex pointed out. "I've never been able to reach the top. **If I blow it again** this year, it could knock me right out of the competition." He looked really bummed.

"That was before," George said. "You're bigger now. And stronger. This could be the year you do it."

"I hope so," Alex said.

"Go ahead and practice," Louie told George and Alex. "It won't help. **Because I'm going to win.**"

"You said the Space Adventurers Program was for saps," George reminded him. "So why enter the contest?"

"Because I can win. And there's nothing I like more than winning," Louie said. He smiled at George. "Especially if my winning means *you* lose."

George scowled. Louie was **such a jerk**. But the fact that Louie wanted him to lose so badly could mean only one thing. George had to win!

Chapter 3

"Here I go!" George shouted as he shinnied up a lamppost on his way home from school that afternoon. "Cl-climbing is h-hard," he **puffed** halfway up the post. "I'll never complete the rope-climbing challenge," George added as he slid down.

"But you can reach the top," Alex said. "I saw you do it on that **obstacle course** when we visited your dad's army base."

George frowned. He'd reached the top, all right. But he hadn't done it on his own. "That was only because the burp burst out of me," George said. "That burp can make me do *anything*." He started to climb a stop sign.

29

"I never thought I'd say this," Alex replied, "but I almost wish I had a burp that could help me like that."

"Don't say that!" George exclaimed. "Don't even *think* it."

Alex nodded. "You're right. It's just that I want to go to the Space Adventurers Program more than anything."

"There are better ways to get there than burping," George told him. **"Trust me."**

"I'm going to have to focus on my questions," Alex said. "That's where I'll score the most points. Hopefully, my mom will drive me to the library later. There's a book I saw last time I was there called *Spaced Out*. It's got tons of information about outer space."

George climbed a little higher on the stop sign and frowned. Alex sure wanted to win this contest. **It kind of stunk** that

George was competing against his best
friend for the prize. But that's just the
way it was.

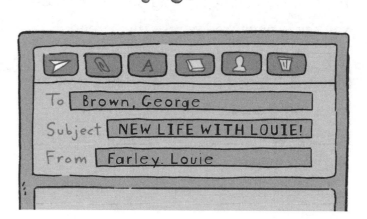

Later that afternoon, George was
staring at Louie's e-mail on his computer
screen. Another *Life with Louie* webisode.
That would be a huge **waste of time**.

George knew he should start working
on his questions for Major Chet Minor.
He hadn't written a single one yet. But he
couldn't help himself. Louie's webisodes

were so. . . . well . . . they were just so *Louie*. Which meant this one was **bound to be hilarious**.

George clicked the link at the bottom of the e-mail. The next thing he knew, **Louie's face** was plastered across the screen.

"Welcome to *Life with Louie!*" Louie shouted. "Today I'm going to show you guys my great workout routine. It's guaranteed to earn me a lot of points during tomorrow's Statewide Physical-Fitness Challenge. Look how strong I am already!"

Louie made a muscle. Or at least he

tried to. All George saw on the screen was Louie's **scrawny arm**, with a **teeny, tiny** bump where the muscle was supposed to be.

"I'm going to show you how many toe-touches I can do," Louie said. He looked into the camera. "Make sure you get me from my best angles," he told the cameraman.

"You got it, Louie," the cameraman said. George was pretty sure it was Mike's voice.

"Now I **bend down** like this . . ." Louie bent over and disappeared from view. All George could see on the screen were Louie's brother Sam's trophies on a shelf as Mike took the camera and circled around.

A moment later, George got **a close-up view of Louie's butt**! The top of his crack was peeking out from above his gym shorts.

"That's his best angle, all right!"
George laughed out loud. **This was classic.**

"Get in front of me!" Louie shouted at
Mike. "It's time for push-ups."

Louie dropped to floor, and Mike
focused the camera on his back.

"One . . . two . . ." Louie counted as he
moved up and down. "Notice how good my
form is. I bend my arms, and then I push
them back up again."

"Oof!" Mike gasped. Suddenly, the
screen went blank. George heard a **loud
crash**.

"Ouch!" Louie shouted. "What are you
doing?"

"Sorry. I tripped," Mike said. "I
dropped the camera."

"On my *head*!" Louie groaned. "That
hurt!"

"Sorry," Mike apologized again. Then
he must have picked up the camera,

because Louie's face came back on the screen. There was **a big lump** forming on the side of his head.

"That's just part of my workout routine," Louie said as he stood and pulled up his shorts. "I'm in great shape. **So watch out.** I'm gonna leave everyone in the dust. Especially you, George Brown. When we run that mile, all you're going to see is my back as I run past you."

"I've already seen your back . . . *side!*" George groaned at his computer screen. "Everyone has," he added as he clicked off the webcast.

Grrr. Every kid in the fourth grade was trying to win that contest. But Louie had only picked on him. **Like always.** George had no idea why Louie hated him so much. But he did.

There was no way George was going to let Louie beat him. Not ever. George was going to win that contest, **no matter what** it took. Which meant George was going to have to have the best questions and be in the best shape of anyone in the whole fourth grade. The work had to start now!

George dropped to the floor and started doing sit-ups. One . . . two . . . three . . . four . . .

He flipped over to do some push-ups.
One . . . two . . . three . . . four . . .

Then he dashed into the hallway and
started running up and down the stairs.
Up . . . down . . . Up . . . down . . .

Sweat was pouring down George's face.
His pits were starting to stink. George
didn't care. All he cared about was beating
Louie Farley!

But that would mean climbing to the
top of the rope. How was George supposed
to practice that? There was nothing to
climb on inside his house. Unless . . .

Suddenly, George's eyes landed on
the drapes in the living-room window.

They went all the way up to the ceiling. If he bunched them together real tight, they were sort of **like a rope**.

Quickly, George raced over to the window. He bunched the drapes up, put one hand above the other, and started pulling himself toward the ceiling. Right hand. Left hand. Right. Left. Ri—

Bam! Oomf! George pulled too hard. The drapes **fell** to the floor, bringing George down with them.

His mother came running out of the kitchen. "Oh no! George, what have you done?" she shouted.

George sat there in the **pile**

of drapes. He'd really made a mess of things now. And he couldn't even blame it on a burp.

There wasn't going to be any more **climbing practice**. George was going to have to come up with another way to win the contest.

"Well, George?" his mother demanded. "What do you have to say for yourself?"

George gulped. "Um . . . I think I have to go to the library?"

Chapter 4

"I can't believe someone else **beat me to the library** and checked out *Spaced Out*," Alex complained the next morning as he, George, and Chris walked into the school yard. "I didn't think anyone else knew that book was even there. It's never been checked out any other time I've gone to the library."

George **looked down** at the ground. He knew exactly who had checked the book out. George Brown. But it wasn't entirely his fault.

George hadn't known that the library only had that one copy. He'd just figured Alex had gotten there earlier and checked one out, too. But now that he knew there was just one copy, he was **too embarrassed** to confess that he was the one who had the book.

"Um . . . couldn't you have used a different science book?" George asked him.

"I did," Alex said. "But *Spaced Out* has specific information about supernova remnants that I would have liked to read before writing my questions."

George remembered seeing the chapter on supernovas. **He hadn't understood a bit of it.** It was filled with math problems and big words. Only a kid like Alex could have possibly known what all that meant. Which made George feel doubly bad about beating Alex to the library and taking it out. Especially since it had been Alex's idea in the first place.

It was all Louie's fault. If he hadn't practically dared George to beat him, George never would have stolen Alex's idea to get the book out of the library.

George frowned. He knew that wasn't *exactly* true. Louie hadn't made George go to the library. George had done it all on his own. And that made it **even worse**. What kind of kid does something that rotten to his own best friend? A Louie kind of kid.

Was George turning into *Louie Farley*? Gulp. George could never let that happen.

Maybe there was a way to make things right. George could drop out of the contest. He could rush home, get the book, and give it to Alex. A smart guy like Alex could redo his questions really quickly.

Just then, Louie came running into the school yard with Mike and Max trailing behind. "Hey, George, you ready to lose?" he shouted. "**'Cause I'm gonna beat you.** My dad had his trainer come over last night to make sure I was in shape. And Sam helped me write my questions. You know how smart Sam is, don't you? They may as well declare me the winner right now."

That did it. No way was George dropping out. He couldn't give Louie the satisfaction. Besides, there wasn't *really* much of a chance George could get back to school with the book in time for Alex to change his questions. And with Alex's problem climbing ropes, there was no guarantee he would win even if George did drop out. So what good would it do?

Louie shot George an **evil smile**. "Watch how fast I can climb to the top of the flagpole and touch the Edith B. Sugarman school flag!" Louie ran over to the flagpole and began climbing.

George glanced at Alex. He was **chewing his fingernails into little nubs**. Any minute now, he'd be chewing his actual fingers.

"Come on," George said to Alex and Chris.

"We can practice our climbing, too."

"You guys go ahead," Chris said. He pulled a sketchbook and a pencil out of his backpack. "I want to finish this page of my latest **Toiletman comic book** before the bell rings. I'm on a roll."

"Okay," George said. He smiled at Alex. "It's just you and me, then."

George raced over to the nearest tree and started to **climb up the trunk**. Alex hurried right behind him.

George grabbed on to a tree branch and pulled

himself up. "Come on," he urged his pal. "Keep climbing." George really wanted Alex to be able to reach the top of the rope. Somehow he thought it would make him feel **less guilty**.

"I'm trying." Alex reached for a branch, but his hand missed. "It's no use," he groaned as he dropped to the ground.

Just then, George spotted Principal McKeon racing into the school yard. He crouched down and tried to **hide behind the leaves**. Kids weren't supposed to climb trees at school. He hoped the principal hadn't spotted him.

"Louie Farley, get down from there!" Principal McKeon shouted. "You know better than to climb a flagpole. That's **disrespectful** to our school flag!"

George watched as Louie shinnied down the pole.

"You and I need to have a little chat,"

Principal McKeon said as she **dragged** Louie across the yard by the hand.

George smiled to himself. It was really nice to see someone else **get in trouble** for a change. Particularly if that someone was Louie Farley!

Chapter 5

Huff. Puff. Huff. Puff.

George gasped for air as he approached the finish line during the first part of the Statewide Physical-Fitness Challenge. **Running a mile was hard.** Still, he'd managed to run the whole thing. Which was good.

Unfortunately, Louie had run it faster. **Which was not good.** Because that had earned him an extra point.

Everyone who finished the mile got ten points. But Julianna, who came in first, got three extra points added to her score. Charlie came in second and he got two extra points. Louie had come in third, so he got one extra point.

Which meant Louie was a whole point ahead of George. *Grrr.*

Just then Sage crossed the finish line. She practically crashed into George. Then she threw her arms around his neck. "Hold me up, Georgie," she said, **blinking her eyelashes** up and down. "I feel like I might collapse."

George really hated when Sage called him Georgie. He didn't like her **wrapping her arms around him**, either.

"You ran so fast, Georgie," Sage said.

"Not fast enough," George replied as he wrestled free from her grasp.

"That's okay," Sage said. "You'll get more points in the next part of the challenge."

George gave Sage a funny look. "Why are you rooting for me? Don't you want to win?"

Sage shook her head. "Kids who go to the Space Adventurers Program have to wear uniforms. I don't like uniforms. I like to wear clothes that help me **express my inner self**."

Oh brother. George wished Sage would take her inner and outer selves to the other side of the field, far away from him.

"Okay, everyone," Coach Trainer

announced a few minutes later. "Now
that you've finished running the mile,
let's head into the gym for the rest of the
challenge."

"Look up," Alex said as the fourth-
graders entered the gym. **"There's my
downfall."**

George looked up. There were six long
ropes hanging from the ceiling. And each
one had a bell at the top.

"Those are long ropes," Chris said.

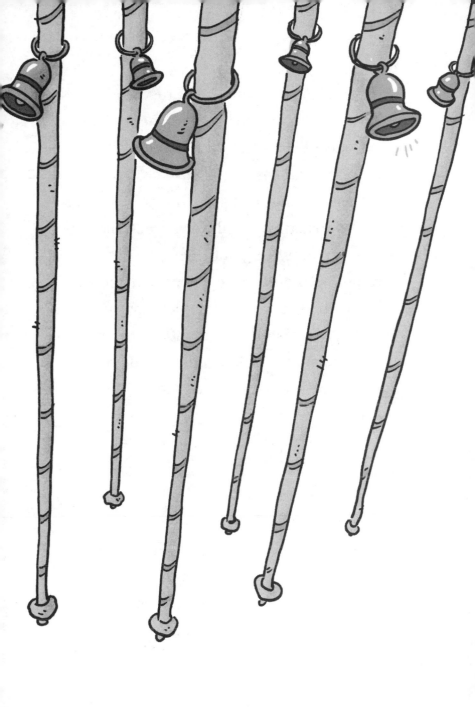

Alex frowned and shook his head. "This is not going to be good," he moaned.

Coach Trainer stood in front of the kids. "You can see that I have set up **stations around the gym**," he said. "Each one is marked with a different activity. For every activity you finish, you get five points. I don't care where you choose to start, but you must complete every activity to finish the challenge. The first person to successfully complete them all gets five extra points added to their score."

Five points. *Wow.* That could change everything.

George looked over at Louie. He had a **weird smile** on his face. Like he had a plan or something that could get him to finish first. Maybe even a plan to cheat.

George had to make sure that didn't happen. He raised his hand.

"Yes, George?" Coach Trainer asked.

"How will you know if someone really did every activity?" George asked.

"There will be a teacher at every station who will put **a check on a chart** next to your name when you finish," Coach Trainer replied.

Just then, the door to the gym opened and some other teachers walked in.

Mrs. Kelly took her place next to the sign that read 10 PUSH-UPS.

The other fourth-grade teacher, Mrs. Miller, stood under the sign that read 35 SIT-UPS.

Ms. Folio, the librarian, stood next to the sign that read 50 TOE-TOUCHES.

Coach Trainer moved over to stand right next to the ropes. "Okay, kids," he said. "**As soon as I blow this whistle, you can start.** One . . . two . . . three!"

At the sound of the whistle, George

hurried to the push-ups station. He **dropped to the floor** and started to move his body up and down. One . . . two . . . three . . .

George knew Louie was doing his push-ups nearby, giving him **the stink eye**. But George didn't look back at Louie. He just tried to stay focused on what he was doing. Eight . . . nine . . . ten.

"Okay, George," Mrs. Kelly said. "You can move on. You too, Louie."

George ran over to the sit-up station and dropped to the floor. He put his hands behind his

head and started crunching. One . . .
two . . . three . . .

George kept going. But suddenly, just
as he reached twenty-nine sit-ups, George
felt something in the bottom of his belly.
Something that had nothing to do with
sit-ups. This was more something like
gas-ups!

George gulped. *Oh no. Not the
burp. Not now. Not in the middle of the
Statewide Physical-Fitness Challenge!*
Somehow, George had to squelch this
belch—**and fast**.

But the bubbles were in really good
shape. They were ping-ponging and
bing-bonging their way through all his
muscles. Already they had trampled
his transverse abdominis, and alley-
ooped over his obliques. Now they were
leapfrogging over his lats and **darting
toward his deltoids**!

George shut his mouth tight, and tried to keep the bubbles from bursting out. And at the same time, he kept doing his sit-ups. Thirty . . . Thirty-one . . .

The bubbles **pounced** on his pecs.

Thirty-two . . . Thirty-three . . . They tripped over his trapezius.

Thirty-four . . . Thirty-five . . .

Chapter 6

Uh-oh. Bubble bubble, **George was in trouble**.

"George, what do you say?" Mrs. Miller asked him.

George looked hopelessly up at the teacher. He opened his mouth to say "Excuse me." But that's not what came out. Instead, George shouted, "Time for toe-touches!"

Before he knew what was happening, George **kicked off his shoes and yanked off his socks**.

"George! What are you doing?" Ms. Folio called to him. "The toe-touch station is over here."

"George, put your shoes back on!" Mrs. Kelly added.

But the burp didn't feel like wearing shoes. It felt like being a **barefoot burp**!

George lay on his back and waved his feet around in the air. One of them landed just under Louie's nose.

"Your feet stink!" Louie shouted to George. "Get them away from me."

No problem! The next thing George knew, he had leaped up in the air and was running over to the toe-touching station. He started bending up and down, touching his toes. One . . . two . . . three . . . four . . .

By the time George reached fifty toe-touches, the burp got tired of counting. So, George took off running around the gym. The kids all stopped what they were doing just to stare at him. Some of them were **holding their noses**, trying not to breathe in George's stinky feet smell.

"George, settle down," Coach Trainer shouted. He blew his whistle.

George wanted to settle down. He really did. But George wasn't in charge anymore. The burp was. And it wanted to **bounce** on a trampoline that Coach Trainer had pushed under the basketball hoop to get it out of the way.

Boing! Boing! Boing! George jumped high in the air. His arms reached up and grabbed the basketball hoop. The next thing George knew, he was **swinging in midair**. His stinky feet were dangling over everyone's head.

"*P.U.*," Louie cried out.

"George, you really need to wash those feet," Julianna agreed.

But the burp didn't care about stinky feet. Burps *like* stink. So George waved his feet in the air, **sending the smell all over the gym**.

Unfortunately, the burp didn't know how to get down from the basketball hoop. The trampoline was no longer there. Coach Trainer had moved it. Again. So the burp just left George hanging there.

George's hands were **getting sweaty**. They were getting slippery. Any minute now he was going to crash to the floor.

Luckily for George, Alex was a much better friend than the burp was. He knew just how to help his pal. Quickly, Alex

rolled a **giant crab soccer** ball across the gym floor. He set it right underneath George. And just in time!

George's sweaty hands slipped their grip. He let go of the hoop and landed feetfirst on top of the giant crab soccer ball.

The ball started to roll—with George standing on top of it.

"George, get down from there!" Coach Trainer shouted as George ran on top of the ball.

George wanted to get down. He really did. But George wasn't the one in control. So George kept running. And the crab soccer ball kept rolling.

George reached

over and **grabbed a hanging rope**.
The next thing George knew, he
was climbing up the rope. His arms
pulled, and his feet pushed. Pull.
Push. Pull. Push. George climbed
higher and higher. He was
almost at the top. And
then . . .

Pop! Suddenly
George felt
something burst
in the bottom
of his belly.
Like someone had
popped a balloon with
a pin. All the air rushed
out of him. The super burp
was gone.

But George was still
there, right near the top of the
rope. So he did the only thing

he could do. He pulled himself up a little higher, reached up, and **rang the bell** at the top of the rope.

Then he slid down and walked over to Coach Trainer.

"I'm finished," George told the phys ed teacher.

"Yes, you are," Coach Trainer agreed. "That was an *unusual* way to get through the stations. But you completed them all. And you were first. **You get five extra points!**"

"Thanks!" George exclaimed. He shot Louie a triumphant smile. Louie shot back a **sore-loser glare**. It was the best dirty look George had ever gotten.

"You still could still win," George told Alex as they walked into the auditorium at the end of the school day. "You got through all of the challenges—even the rope-climbing. And I bet your questions were amazing."

"I can't believe I got to the top of that rope!" Alex said proudly. "I guess all my practicing paid off. Which is awesome, because I don't think I've wanted anything more than this, ever."

"You want this more than getting your picture in the *Schminess Book of World Records* for having the **world's largest already been chewed gumball**?" Chris asked him. "You were pretty excited when that happened."

"This is different," Alex explained. "It was fun collecting all that ABC gum. But science is my life!"

George looked down and kicked guiltily at the ground.

Just then, Mrs. Kelly and Mrs. Miller walked onto the stage. Mrs. Kelly was holding a piece of paper in her hand.

"This is it!" Alex said. He crossed his fingers, his arms, and his ankles. For a second, George thought he saw Alex try to **cross his eyes**. Boy, did he want to win.

"We've gone over everyone's questions and added up your scores," Mrs. Miller said. "It was very close."

"There were some **remarkable** questions," Mrs. Kelly added.

George thought she looked at Alex when she said that. Alex must have thought so, too, because he sat up a little taller.

"But we can only have **one winner**,"
Mrs. Miller said. "And one student had good
questions plus a strong score on the physical
challenge. And that student is . . ."

The kids all leaned forward in their seats.

"George Brown!" Mrs. Kelly shouted excitedly. "George, come on up here and take a bow."

Mrs. Kelly didn't have to ask twice. George leaped up from his seat and raced up onto the stage. The other fourth-graders clapped for him. Well, all except for Louie.

"No fair!" Louie shouted. "I could have finished the challenge first. **But I got all woozy from George's stinky feet.** George only won because he took off his shoes."

George knew Louie was half right. He hadn't won all on his own. The magical super burp had actually helped him for once. But no one knew that, except Alex.

George glanced over to where Alex

was sitting. He was clapping his hands and trying really hard to look happy for his best pal.

Which just made **George feel more rotten** about getting to the library before him.

But George couldn't say anything about that. Or about the burp. Because that would mean telling everyone that he was a rotten friend who was followed around by a magical super burp. And there was no way George was doing that.

Chapter 7

Ding-dong.

"I'll get it," George shouted. He raced down the stairs at top speed and peeked out the window to see who was there.

"Hey, Alex," George said as he opened the door. "What are you doing here?"

"Hi," Alex answered. "I had something I wanted to give you for **your interview** tomorrow."

George looked down at the ground.

"It's okay," Alex told him. "If I couldn't win, I'm glad you did."

"Thanks," George said.

"Anyway, I came over to give you these," Alex said. He handed George a plastic bag filled with **brownish-red candies**.

"Um . . . thanks?" George was confused. What were those things?

"They're ginger candies," Alex explained. "There was a post on the Burp No More Blog that said ginger coats your stomach and **stops gas** from building up. And no gas means . . ."

"No burps," George said, finishing Alex's thought. He popped one of the candies in his mouth. "Ow!" he exclaimed. **"That's spicy."**

"I know," Alex told George. "You can't eat too many at once. But I figured if you ate a ginger candy right before your interview with Major Minor, you wouldn't burp on camera."

"I've been worrying about that," George admitted.

"The interview is definitely the scary part," Alex said. "I don't think I could do it. Just knowing that the whole school was watching me would probably **make me freeze**."

"But your questions were probably a whole lot smarter than mine," George said.

Alex reached into his pocket and pulled out **a piece of paper**. "Here are the questions I turned in. If you run out of things to ask, and there's still time left, you can ask Major Minor one of these."

"Wow!" George exclaimed. "Thanks. You want to come in and hang out?"

"Just for a little bit," Alex said as he walked into George's living room. "I told my mom I wouldn't be . . . *Hey, what's that?*"

George glanced in the direction Alex was looking.

"*You're* the guy who checked out *Spaced Out*?" Alex demanded, staring at the book on the living-room table. "After I told you I was going to do that? **Why would you do that to me?**"

George didn't know what to say. "I didn't do it to you," he mumbled finally. **"I did it to Louie.** He kept saying he was going to win, and then on his webcast he . . ."

George babbled on and on. But Alex wasn't listening.

"Louie didn't use his best friend's idea to help him win," Alex interrupted. "You did. You knew how bad I wanted to go to the Space Adventurers Program. You never even heard of it before the other day. That was **a crummy thing to do**, George." And with that, Alex stormed out of George's house.

George kicked at the ground as the door slammed. He felt really, really rotten. Alex was right. **He was a crummy friend.** The absolute crummiest.

George thought about Alex all night long. He was the guy who should be talking to Major Minor tomorrow. Not George. Alex had entered the contest because he was genuinely interested in space. Not just in **winning some contest** or beating Louie Farley.

George turned off the light and climbed into bed. He shut his eyes and tried to sleep. But he couldn't. His mind was racing way too fast. And he wasn't just thinking about Alex. There were

other things to worry about, too.

Like, George couldn't believe his
mom was making him wear a tie. **A TIE!**
He wasn't going to look like the perfect
example of a fourth-grader. He was going to
look **like a geek**!

What if he woke up in the morning with
laryngitis, and nothing but squeaks came
out of him?

Or what if **a big pimple** sprouted on his
nose overnight?

Or what if he fell off his chair right
when he was asking Major Minor an
important question?

And the biggest *what if* of all—what
if the ginger candies didn't work and
the burp **exploded** right in Major
Minor's face? What kind of
trouble would happen then?
What if? What if?
What if?

Suddenly, George heard a **strange whirring noise** coming from outside. He opened his eyes and looked around.

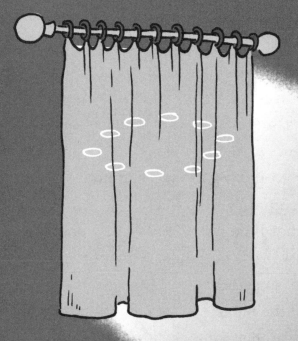

There were green and red lights flashing through the windows. Which would have made sense if it was Christmastime. But it wasn't.

What was going on?

George **leaped** out of his bed. He raced to the window. The red and green lights were spinning around and around. The whirring was getting louder and louder.

And then, suddenly . . . *whoosh*! The flashing lights and whirring noises disappeared. **And so did George Brown!**

Chapter 8

"Get off me!" George shouted. He shoved the **tiny green men** who had planted themselves on his shoulder to the ground. Then he grabbed the one who was sitting on his head by the antenna and yanked him off.

"Get away!" George shouted again.

Wait a minute. Tiny green men? **Antenna?** What was going on here?

George looked around. This wasn't his bedroom. It couldn't be. There was no bed. Besides, George's bedroom wasn't round. It didn't have big computer screens on the walls. It didn't have all kinds of buttons and knobs on the desks. And it didn't have hundreds of little green men running all around.

This was no bedroom. This was a **spaceship**! George was sure of it. He'd seen them in the movies a million times. Only they didn't seem so scary then.

"AAAAAHHHHHH!" George screamed.

At the sound of George's voice, hundreds of little green faces turned in his direction. **Their red eyes began to glow.** And they all started talking at once.

George couldn't understand a word they were saying. To him it sounded like Mrs. Kelly giving a science lesson. *Blah blah blah.* Only their voices were **squeakier** than Mrs. Kelly's. And they weren't giving him gummy smiles.

"AAAAAHHHHHH!" George screamed again.

A group of little green men started climbing up on one another's shoulders. They were making a little green tower. The little man at the top of the tower reached into George's mouth and started **counting his teeth**. Weird. He was like a little green dentist!

At the same time, another little green man was counting George's toes. At least he was, until he took **one whiff** of George's stinky feet. That stink was so bad it even made an alien run away!

Another alien was counting George's fingers, while another was listening to his heart with a **teeny tiny stethoscope**. Suddenly, George understood what going on. These little green men were trying to figure out what made George tick.

Or make that *tickle*. Because now one of them was poking George in the belly with his little green hand. And boy, did that tickle.

"Hahahahaha!" George laughed so hard it knocked the **tower of little green men** to the ground. They scattered around their spaceship and began pushing all sorts of buttons and knobs.

George took a deep breath. These

little green men didn't seem scary. **They actually seemed friendly.** They didn't want to hurt him. They just wanted to learn about him.

Wait until Louie heard about this! The aliens didn't want to study one of the Farley brothers. They wanted to study *George*—a perfect example of a fourth-grade boy.

George was kind of curious about the little green men, too. And about their spaceship. All those **buttons and knobs** seemed really cool.

Blah blah blah . . .

All of a sudden, a bunch of the little green men started speaking and pointing. But George had no idea what they were talking about until they jumped up on one of the desks and lined up to form **a green arrow**. The arrow was pointing to a knob.

They wanted him to push the knob. So

that's exactly what George did. A little door opened, and a bowl of **chocolate ice cream** slid out. Wow!

The little green arrow, made of little green men, shifted to the right. Now they were pointing to a switch. So George pulled the switch. Chocolate syrup rained down on the ice cream.

The little green arrow moved to the left. Now it was pointing to a lever. George pulled the lever. Suddenly something that looked like **a laser gun** popped out.

A laser gun? *Gulp.* What if George had been wrong? What if these little green men *weren't* friendly? What if that laser was going to disintegrate George?

What if? What if? What if?

Whoosh! Just then, **whipped cream shot out** of the laser gun. It landed on top of the ice cream and chocolate sauce. Phew. A little whipped cream never hurt anyone.

A space-age sundae! George couldn't wait to take a taste.

The space aliens couldn't wait for him to take a taste, either. They were standing around with their **bright red glowing eyes** staring right at him.

Unfortunately, there was one thing missing: a spoon. But that didn't stop George. He just stuck his mouth into that ice-cream sundae and began **slurping** it up. What a fun way to eat a sundae!

95

What a *messy* way to eat a sundae! Ice cream, whipped cream, and chocolate sauce were dripping all over George's face. George didn't see any napkins, so he wiped **his mouth on his sleeve**. In space, no one can tell you to have manners.

George looked out one of the big round windows. He could still see his house. But it was starting to look far, far away. The spaceship was on the move. **George was heading into outer space.**

WHOA! Suddenly, George's feet lifted off the ground.

BASH! His head banged into the roof of the spaceship. His body twisted and turned in the air. He tried to force his feet back down, but that just made him flip over and do a **somersault** in midair.

No matter what he did, George couldn't touch the ground. That's what happens

when you travel around in *zero gravity*.

Which could only mean one thing. **The spaceship was flying away.** Out of the Earth's atmosphere!

It was one thing when these space aliens wanted him to come onboard and share ice cream with them. That was fine, as long as George could still see his house from the spaceship window. But now his house just looked like a **tiny little dot**.

At least George thought that was his house. It was hard to tell. All the houses on the ground looked like tiny little dots.

Gulp. This was *ba-a-ad*.

What if the aliens wanted him to travel with them to their planet? That could take a long, long time. Living in space could be rough. Who was George supposed to talk to? **He didn't speak space alien.**

What was he supposed to eat? Chocolate sundaes were delicious, but a guy could get tired of them eventually.

Speaking of tired, what if George wanted to go to sleep? There didn't seem to be any beds on board the spaceship.

Worse yet, sooner or later, George was going to have to **go to the bathroom**. With all this zero gravity, George wondered, how do you pee in space?

"I WANT TO GO HOME!" George cried out suddenly.

The little green men all turned and stared at him. **Their red eyes flashed.** Their tiny mouths opened. And then . . . they all started laughing.

George shook his head. This wasn't funny. Not at all.

And it was about to get a lot worse. Those aliens wouldn't be laughing if they knew that there was an **uninvited guest** on board their spaceship. The kind of guest that was bound to cause trouble. *Bubble* trouble!

Chapter 9

Bling-blong! Pling-plong!

The super burp was back. And it wanted out! Already it was pouncing on George's pancreas and belly-flopping onto his bladder. George couldn't let the burp loose on a spaceship. There was no telling what it would do here. **He had to squelch the belch.**

But how?

If George were on Earth he might have stood on his head and hoped the bubbles would travel up into his feet. That had worked before.

Or he might have started **spinning around and around**

until the burp swirled back down to his toes like **water going down the drain**. That had been a good belch squelcher, too. But would it work in zero gravity? George had absolutely no idea.

Plink-plonk. Zink-zonk! The bubbles were tickling his tonsils, tiptoeing their way up onto his tongue, and traipsing between his teeth. And then . . .

George let out a burp. A super burp. A burp so strong and so loud it could be heard **on the moon**—which was actually a lot closer to him now than it used to be.

The magical super burp was on the loose in *outer space*. George opened his mouth to say "Excuse me." But that's not what came out. Instead he shouted, "Loop de loop!"

The next thing George knew, he was **doing cartwheels** in space. Flip. Flip. Flip. George's body spun around and around. And his feet never once touched the ground.

The little green men started chattering at once.

"Leapfrog!" George shouted suddenly. He started leaping over little green men. Hop! Hop! Hop!

The little green men **scattered** as fast as they could. But they weren't fast enough. Before even George knew what was happening, he had reached out his hand and **scooped up** three of them.

"Juggle!" George shouted. He started juggling the three little green men in the air.

George was not a good juggler. The burp had made him do this before, with raw eggs in the middle of the classroom. That hadn't gone so well. In fact it had been **a major mess**.

It was no wonder the little green men

had such frightened looks on their little green faces. George was dropping them. One, two, three.

The only good thing was, with zero gravity, they didn't hit the ground. **They just floated away.**

The burp turned its attention to the buttons on the desks that lined the spaceship. George's hand reached out and pulled the chocolate-syrup switch. Chocolate syrup rained down in the spaceship.

Then George pulled the whipped-cream lever. The whipped-cream laser gun started shooting.

George's hand reached over and pushed a yellow button. **Rainbow sprinkles** rained from the sky.

The little green men looked at one another. They chattered loudly. They sounded scared.

George wanted to tell the little green men not to be scared. The burp was crazy, yes. But it wasn't mean. It wouldn't hurt anyone. At least not on purpose.

But the burp didn't feel like talking. It felt like **squirting whipped cream** all around the spaceship. So George just kept pulling that lever.

Bonk! Just then, George felt something hit him in the back of the head. *Bonk! Bonk! Bonk!*

George swiveled around. Cherries! The little green men were **launching cherries** at him. And their aim was really good!

George squirted some whipped cream back at the little green men. It was an all-out, **outer-space ice-cream war**!

George leaped up high to avoid being hit with a cherry bomb. "Incoming!" George shouted as he **flip-flopped and loop-de-looped** out of the way of flying cherries.

Bonk! Bonk! Two cherries hit their mark. Right in the middle of George's forehead.

"Oh yeah?" George shouted. "Well, take this!" His hand reached for **a bright red button**.

George had no idea what the red button would do. But the space aliens seemed to know. And they weren't happy.

"AAAAAAAHHHHH!" the little green men shouted as they scurried to stop George from pushing the button. Some pulled at his arm. Some pulled at his legs.

But **the burp was stronger** than all of them! It forced George's hand on the bright red button and pushed.

Beep! Beep! Beep! An alarm sounded. Bright red lights **flashed** everywhere! The little green men took cover. And then . . .

Pop! Suddenly, George felt something pop inside his belly. All the air rushed out of him. **The magical super burp was gone.**

Beep! Beep! Beep!

And his alarm was ringing.

What? George opened his eyes and looked around. There was his desk. And his chair. And his skateboard. And his backpack.

Yep. This was his room. He hadn't gone anywhere. **It had all been a dream.**

But it had been so real. That ice cream had tasted sweet and been so cold. And he'd definitely felt every one of those cherry bombs bash into his head.

George looked down at his sleeve. Hey! What was that **brown stuff**? It looked like chocolate sauce.

No. That was impossible. It couldn't
be chocolate sauce. Because there were
no such things as outer-space sundaes or
little green men.

There couldn't be.

Could there?

Chapter 10

"We're on the air in one minute," said Jason, the fifth-grader who was directing Thursday's morning announcements.

George and Major Minor were seated **in front of the camera** in the school TV studio. But George's mind was far away. Far, far away. In outer space. George was still thinking about the space aliens.

"I'm ready," Major Chet Minor said with a smile. **"How about you, George?"**

"Huh?" George asked.

"Are you ready?" Major Minor repeated.

"Oh. Yeah. Sure. I guess," George answered.

"Okay," Jason said. "We're on the air."

George looked at the camera. Its red light looked like a little green man's eye. He would never forget those eyes. Ever. **They were real.** He was sure of it.

"Do you believe in space aliens?" George blurted out suddenly.

The words were out of George's mouth before he could stop them. And boy, was he sorry he'd ever said them. Louie would never let him live this down. George looked like **an idiot**.

Except . . . Major Minor wasn't laughing at him. He was actually nodding! "I think it's possible that there's life on other planets," he said. "Maybe not life as we know it. But some form of life. In fact, NASA has pictures that show the ice caps on Mars, caps with ice made of water. And where there's water, there could be life."

"Wow!" George exclaimed. So it *was* possible that there were little green men somewhere. And if that was true, then George had something else to ask Major Minor. Something that had been really bugging him since last night.

"How do you pee in space?" George asked the astronaut.

"When you gotta go, you gotta go," Major Minor joked. Then he explained, "We have toilets that look pretty much like the ones on Earth. But we don't flush with water. We use air pressure to **pull waste** through the system."

George grinned. It turned out that it was an interesting question to ask. But it wasn't a really *smart* question. And George wanted Major Minor to think

he was smart. So he asked one of Alex's super-smart questions.

"Do neutron stars or white dwarf stars have enough mass to eventually become **black holes**?" George asked Major Minor.

Major Minor looked at him with surprise. "Wow!" he exclaimed. "What a great question."

George beamed.

Major Minor started discussing things like measuring mass, black holes, and something called event horizons. George had no idea what he was talking about. He doubted any of the other kids in school, except Alex, would understand either.

Finally, Major Minor finished answering the question. He smiled. "You must be a **top science student**, George," he said. "Just the kind of kid we love at the Space Adventurers Program."

George looked at the ground. It was

one thing to use Alex's question. After all, Alex had given it to him and told him to use it. But it was another thing to take credit for Alex's brains. **That was something he just couldn't do.**

"Actually, it was my friend Alex who came up with that question," George admitted. "He loves science. And he really wanted to go to the Space Adventurers Program. Even more than I did. So if it's okay, I'm going to give him that part of my prize."

Major Minor didn't say anything for a minute. Then he reached out and shook George's hand. "You're acting like **a real astronaut**," he said.

Huh?

"Astronauts are loyal to one another, and you're obviously loyal to your friend Alex," Major Minor explained. "And **astronauts have to use teamwork** when

they're in space. Alex shared his question
with you, and that's teamwork. I think
you both should get to go to the Space
Adventures Program. *Together*. So I'm
going to make sure both you boys get a
scholarship to the program."

"**Really?**" George asked him.

Major Minor grinned. "Really," he said.

"Thanks!" George exclaimed.

Just then, Jason held up five fingers.
There were only five seconds left in the
broadcast.

"**Thank you, Major Minor**, for being

on our morning announcements," George said into the camera. "The fourth-graders will get to hear more from you at their assembly today."

"And we're out," James said as the **little red light** on the camera faded. "Thanks for a good show, everyone."

As George and Major Minor left the studio, Alex came racing down the hall.

"What are you doing here?" George asked Alex.

"Mrs. Kelly said I could come thank Major Minor for the **scholarship** in person," Alex told him.

"Oh," George said.

"And to thank you, too," Alex said. "That was **a cool thing** you did, dude."

"Well, you are my best friend," George said hopefully.

"Definitely," Alex replied.

George smiled and looked up at Major Minor. "This is Alex," he said. **"The kid I was telling you about."**

"Nice to meet you, Alex," Major Minor said. "That was an interesting question you wrote."

"Thanks," Alex said. "I liked your answer. It made a lot of things clearer for me. And I was wondering if I could

ask you a few more things before the assembly."

"Sure," Major Minor said. "Ask away."

George smiled as he listened to Alex and the astronaut talk about things George could never possibly understand. He was glad Alex had a chance to get his

questions answered. Especially because the only other question George would have wanted to ask, **he already knew the answer to**.

At one time, George might have wondered if it was possible to burp in space. But he'd already done that last night, in the alien spaceship. So he definitely knew it was possible.

At least, he thought he knew. George couldn't be completely sure. Because he couldn't be completely sure he'd actually been inside an alien spaceship. **It might have been a dream.**

Maybe.

But then again, maybe not.

About the Author

Nancy Krulik is the author of more than 150 books for children and young adults, including three *New York Times* Best Sellers and the popular Katie Kazoo, Switcheroo books. She lives in New York City with her family, and many of George Brown's escapades are based on things her own kids have done. (No one delivers a good burp quite like Nancy's son, Ian!) Nancy's favorite thing to do is laugh, which comes in pretty handy when you're trying to write funny books! You can follow Nancy on Twitter: @NancyKrulik.

About the Illustrator

Aaron Blecha was raised by a school of giant squid in Wisconsin and now lives with his family by the south English seaside. He works as an artist designing funny characters and illustrating humorous books, including the one you're holding. You can enjoy more of his weird creations at www.monstersquid.com.